# JACKEL BUNNY

## BY

## KEVIN DAVIS

ISBN: 979-8-89778-373-1 (Paperback)

# Preface

The once-quiet road that led to Syfer Keep was now little more than a dirt walk that was overgrown with bushes and shrubbery. The streets of the town are littered with broken branches and leaves, and the overgrown gardens' tall grasses wave in the breeze. As rust destroyed their edges, many doors had crumbled. Open doorways, which may have formerly been extremely hospitable, were now a spooky and unwelcoming appearance. In some situations, the only indication of a fire was a smoke and soot trail above a window, while in other cases, it was a pile of ash where a building had once been. Syfer Keep, which was once a peaceful community with kind residents, had vanished into obscurity.

The numerous voices of a formerly vibrant population were replaced by the numerous voices of stray dogs and wild animals who had moved into this town as their new home. The water in the community pool was still full. Rainwater that is tainted with algae. Although it was large enough to accommodate several duck families, even they eerily abandoned it. The village has a particular allure despite the state of the structures. As nature became more untamed, everything became greener, and the daytime silence was nearly serene. You couldn't help, but feel that so much had been gone for good, even with all the creatures that now called this place home.

# Chapter 1

Nobody survives life unharmed. Perhaps all of the devil's plans paled in comparison to what man might concoct. The monsters that came back to life pale in comparison to the ones we carry within. Never rely on what you hear, and only take in half of what you see. Deception is your biggest enemy, especially when your mind is not properly trained to face tough tasks at hand. Ideally, you won't see Heaven. I'm here to guide you to the other shore, into never-ending darkness, fire, and ice. "Hey Amya!" A young man asks a quiet girl who is concentrating on her work in the college park. As he walks over to her patiently and not trying to scare her as she has her headphones on. "Amya!" He says while touching her shoulder which ends up making her jump. "Omg! What the fuck Chris?" Amya reacts to Chris. Chris smiles and laughs as he apologizes to Amya, "Sorry about that I called you on your phone first, but no answer. Plus I called you while I was walking over here. When I saw you under this tree."

A lovely, melancholy face is hung awkwardly over by golden, wavy hair. A blazing recollection of a tremendous reputation is left behind by her glinting violet eyes, scars that extend from just under her right eye, continue towards her left nostril, and stop under her left eye. This is Amya Katherine Fitsgerald's face. She has an odd quality about her; it might be a sense of embarrassment or it might just be pure delight. However, people frequently pose as her closest friends while really just wishing to fight alongside her.

Lengthy, black hair that is perfectly coiffed reveals a long, aged face. An intriguing reminder of his fortunate history is left by the mark of gentle brown eyes and running thin lips. This is Christopher Barnfield's appearance. Who excels as a quarterback in football, but who is also the best buddy anyone could ask for. While wishing for a comeback in the acting world eventually.

"Ok! So what do you want Chris? It seems I've not been a priority to you for the past few weeks, since your season started." Amya explains to Chris how she feels neglected by him since football season began. They have been bestfriends since they were in elementary school. They have been inseparable for a long time. After going through elementary to high school together, when college started things took a turn. "I'm sorry Amya... I've been caught up and everything is changing so fast. I don't mean to make you feel this way. How about this...there's a celebration tonight since today is Halloween and I want you to come. What do you say?" Amya hesitates to respond.... And finally says, "College parties tend to get out of hand, especially with alcohol. But you lucky I love and trust you. Where is it going to be?" Chris dances with excitement and says, "It's going to be at my new apartment I just got in Rudwick County. I can swing by your dorm and pick you up if you like." Amya agrees to do this with Chris and he walks off with a smile on his face. As he leaves Amya continues to listen to her music, but gets distracted by a woman across the park from her. The woman

seems to be wearing a bloody bunny mask, and a

black dress with sneakers. It appears as the woman

is sitting in a chair looking directly at Amya. Amya,

confused by how everyone is not reacting, is

wondering if she is seeing things. People continue to

walk past this bloody bunny masked figure woman

with no attention to see about her. Amya quickly

packs up her back pack and rushes to her dorm and

turns around to see the woman is no longer in sight.

Sabrina Jackel and Jackel Bunny

# Chapter 2

Being able to see, but blind is the worst possible situation. Even though the once-bright light has been permanently removed from the view. Even so, nothing can bring back the moment of beauty in the flower and splendor in the grass. Instead of mourning, we shall draw strength from what is still there. Time is like a river of passing events, and its stream is swift. As soon as something is brought to our attention, it is gone, replaced by something else, which will soon follow. Rejoice, for your spirit is alive, if the sight of the blue skies brings you delight, if the strength of a blade of grass emerging in the fields can move you, or if the straightforward messages of nature speak to you. Even complete strangers might occasionally catch our attention right away, without us even exchanging a word. The time has come for the darkness in the skies has arisen. It can be seen that a couple of friends embark to have the time of their lives at a local gas station store. "Yo!! Bro you ready for the party tonight man. We are about to be lit!" One of Chris' friends says in the store while picking out drinks and snacks to eat. "Hell yeah man, I just have to swing by and get my friend Amya from her dorm first." Chris says in response to his friend that goes by the name of Jolt Phillips. "Yeah, friend of course man I see you." Jolt winks at Chris as he believes Amya is someone more than just a friend.

As they are cracking jokes and looking for snacks, one of the other friends named Tanner looks over at the cashier to see a woman in a black dress and leather jacket. A young, anxious face is nearly completely hidden by shoulder-length, black hair and sparkly blue eyes. His nose is charmingly complemented by his dark beard, which also beautifully recalls his privileged childhood. This is the physique of Jolt Philips. Tanner Yung has a narrow, warm face that is obscured by neatly styled black hair that drapes uncomfortably. Aquamarine eyes with hollow sockets that are firmly seated. His fair skin gracefully enhances the beauty of his mouth and creates an unforgettable impression of his miraculous survival. Tanner is known as the most kind hearted one of the group and the most curious.

"Yo! Tanner, what are you looking at bro?" Chris asked. "Oh! Wait a minute you are looking at that beautiful woman over there. How about you don't look like a creepy dude and go make a conversation." Chris continued teasing Tanner. "She's way out of my league, I doubt she would even want to talk to me." Tanner says calmly. Jolt laughs at Tanner and yells out to the woman in black and says "Hey! Excuse me ma'am, my boy over here has a crush on you!!" Tanner and Chris both shout, "Dude, what the hell is your problem?" The woman in black seems to be flattered and appears to look at tanner in a flirty way as she walks out the door. Tanner then runs after her outside to apologize for the actions of Jolt. "Ma'am I am so sorry about that, my friend really has no home training at all. Please forgive his actions." The woman in black responds to Tanner with, "You jocks are always the same, no matter in high school or college. You lucky you cute tho. What is your name?"

Tanner smiles after the compliment was said and says, "My name Tanner... What's your name?" The woman in black seductively rubs on Tanner's chest and tells him her name... "Sabrina Jackel is my name sweetheart. Would you like to get out of here and go somewhere with me?"

Tanner hesitates, but is convinced to go with Sabrina as she continues to rub his body. Meanwhile, Chris and Jolt are looking out and watching the conversation going on. Jolt smiles hysterically saying, "Oh Snap! Our boy is about to get laid oh yeah!! Man I'm kind of jealous tho." Chris looks at Jolt as he believes Jolt is an idiot… "Jolt shut the hell up and go pay for this stuff. I'll be in the car." Tanner is persuaded to go with Sabrina and says, "Let me go tell my friends and I'll meet you at your car." Sabrina smiles and leads Tanner to her car, "Sweet! My car is at pump 13." Tanner is aroused and excited when he sees her car, "Oh shit you have a red mercedes. That's dope, I'll be there." With all excitement coursing through Tanner's veins, he runs to Chris to tell him the news. Tanner knocks on the door window of Chris. Chris says, "What's up bro! What's happening?" Tanner smiles, "Dude!! Ummm… she invited me to go with her." Chris seems concerned, "Invited you to go where exactly man. You don't even know her. Are you sure about this?" Chris is the big brother of the group and always watches out for everyone he is close to. "I know it seems shady, but I think she is fine bro.. I appreciate you for always looking out, but I think I'll be fine."

Chris contemplates Tanner's decision, but he lets him go. "Well I'm not your dad or anything, just be careful. Have fun brother." Tanner runs off excited with no care in the world. As Tanner takes off with Sabrina, Jolt finally decides to come with all the items for the party. "It's about damn time you came out bruh. Let's get out of here " Chris frustratingly says. "Alright man and I see Tanner is about to get him some. That's my boy." Chris looks annoyed and is ready to just punch Jolt in the face.

Things that seem the most

innocent are the most deadly

-Kevin Davis

Helping others would be just as good, but even if you could, you wouldn't. Meeting a stranger, for instance, might be completely pointless until you enter their world by learning at least one thing about their lives that is significant to them. Exchanging at least one genuine sentiment. You send yourself out toward people, and you receive them as they respond to you when you are tuned in to them. Life is like taking the bus. When we get on the bus, the trip officially starts. Along the road, we run into a variety of people—some are strangers, others are friends, and some strangers are yet to become friends.  At regular intervals, pauses are made, and passengers board. Some of these folks occasionally make themselves known and have an impression on us fellow passengers by their grace and beauty. While other times they are completely uninterested. Sometimes it's necessary for people to leave, to get down, and proceed along the paths they were meant to travel. If everyone made an entrance and never left, for better or worse, we would feel trapped and bewildered like the passengers in the bus. The journey's purpose would be obscured, and the trip wouldn't be satisfying or easy overall.

On the ride with Sabrina Jackel, Tanner is nervous, but excited. This is his first time being with anyone other than his friends. "Why do you seem so nervous, you think I'm going to bite you or something?" Sabrina asks Tanner with a sadistic nervous smile on her face as she drives. Tanner attempts to laugh his nervousness off as they ride down a dark street.

Nothing, forest trees and dark clouds can be seen as they ride down the highway.

"I am a bit nervous, because I've never been with anyone outside my friend group. I keep my circle small, because I trust no one. I took a leap of faith with you, because I think you are really hot and also to brag to my friends." Tanner explains to Sabrina.

"Where are we headed tho? We are like in the middle of nowhere?" Tanner begins to be concerned about his decision making.

Sabrina begins to harmonize disturbingly and rocks her head, while driving to their destination. "What are you humming? Why aren't you answering my questions?.... This shit is starting to get creepy as fuck now. Turn back around and take me back."

Sabrina is not caring to listen to Tanner plead for his life as he is terrified out of his mind.

After a thirty minute to an hour drive on a dark road, Sabrina parks the car at a house in the forest. The outside of this house is stunning. It contains ornamentation made of brown brick and was constructed with white stones. Short, wide windows have been symmetrically added to the house, adding to its overall design. The home offers a lovely living room, four bedrooms, a spacious dining space, a multimedia room, and a small storage room in addition to a tiny kitchen and one huge bathroom. The structure has a brief U-shaped form. To either side, the two extensions expand into textile sunscreens. Due to the second floor's lesser size than the first, the home has multiple tiny balconies on one side. Compared to the floor below, this floor has a radically different aesthetic.

Brown roof tiles are used to cover the low, pyramid-shaped roof. The middle of the roof is punctured by two little chimneys. The chambers below the roof were well-lit thanks to the numerous smaller windows.  A modest garden with largely grass and a few small trees surrounds the home.

"Where are we?" Tanner asks Sabrina as she gets out of the car and goes inside the house even though it looks deserted. She briefly turns around at Tanner with a devilish smile and asks, "Well are you coming in? It's time to party. My friends are inside. Don't be afraid." Sabrina leaves Tanner in the car as she walks inside the house. Tanner slowly gets out of the car and questions himself, "What the hell am I doing?

What friends is she talking about? This house looks like a murder or even suicide house. Dear God forgive me for I have sinned and If I die tonight I hope you take my soul." Meanwhile Tanner contemplates his life with Sabrina. Amya is in her dorm room waiting for Chris to come pick her up and head to the party celebration in Rudwick County. Rudwick county is an hour outside of Syfer Keep.

The city of Rudwick County, which is constantly expanding, was constructed amidst the murky waters of a sizable swamp. The backdrop of clear skies, which have helped mold the city into what it is now, matches its elegance.  The environment that these skies delivered was very significant, but they also had an impact on architectural styles because the vast majority of structures were built to make the most of the climate by having expansive windows and rich landscaping. Luxurious skyscrapers are adding to the city's skyline, and each one seems to change with the times without losing sight of its past. Rudwick County is experiencing a rise in culture, which has drawn considerable attention. A few foreign cultures have had an impact on the city's identity as well as on business. What was once a metropolis of monotony has developed into a new culture of variety, and it is this that still binds the 6 million residents of the city together today. "Oh! So who are you dressing up for? Girl you actually look like a human in your jeans and that's a pink shirt on. Oh my god, it's not a raggedy shirt that makes you look homeless" Alyssia tells Amya. "Oh girl stop, you know I like to dress comfortably, but tonight

Imma going to do something different. Chris invited me to a party in Rudwick County and he's my bestfriend I have to go. Only because I trust him." Amya replies.

Only the current moment offers the possibility of life. You cannot really experience the moments of your daily life if you ignore the present. Instead than lamenting the past, fretting about the future, or preparing for problems, the key to mental and physical health is to make the most of the present moment. Amya is strong-willed, stubborn, impulsive, and petulant. This isn't shocking given who she is and her troubled past.

She was raised in a working-class family in a run-down town where she was born and raised. Up until the age of about 8, she enjoyed a comfortable life, but then things started to go south. She was abandoned by everyone when her parents fled during an uprising. She had to live in a wild world with a relative, Alyssia, her roommate. She was able to stay ahead of the curve and exceed expectations thanks to her intelligence and knowledge, though. She became the woman she is now as a result of this. "You know you are my cousin and of course I have to always tease you. So is Chris on the way now?" Alyssa continues with Amya. "Indeed he is…" Amya says as her phone dings in the middle of the conversation when Chris messages her that he and Jolt are outside now. "Well actually he's here and waiting outside for me. How do I look?" With all her introvertness Amya seems to be excited for this party. "You look dashing Amya, now go have fun." Alyssia encourages Amya.

Amya walks out her door when Alyssia receives a text message from a private number. The number saying, "Is the package on the way yet?" Alyssia simply replies, "Yes! I can't believe you made me do this."

# What did Alyssia Do???

# Chapter 4

Silent, stone secrets dwell in the deep chambers of our respective hearts: secrets are tired of their oppression: tyrants who are ready to be overthrown. If we could learn the hidden past of our adversaries, we should discover enough agony and misery in each man's life to end all hostilities.

Chris steps out of the car and waits outside of Amya's dorm room building for her arrival. Meanwhile Jolt is impatient and complaining about when she is showing up. "Dude why do females take so freaking long.. Like come on." Chris politely walks over to Jolt and punches him in the face.. "How about you shut the fuck up and be patient. Gosh you are so fucking annoying. I sometimes wonder how I even became friends with you." Jolt holds his nose, "Dammit bro you didn't have to hit me."

Jolt nose starts to bleed, so he rushes to go find a restroom to clean himself up. Amya makes her down to see Chris and jumps with happiness. "Wow, you seem really joyful." Chris says as he hugs Amya. "You didn't seem like this earlier when I first came to you." Chris continued. "Well, you know earlier I was in deep thoughts about stuff, but you are my best friend and I'm so excited to hang out with you. It's been too long." Amya explained. "Well awesome I'm happy too and I have to warn Jolt is with me too. Only because this is his car." Chris exclaimed. Amya responds, "Ok, but where is he?" Chris turns around quickly with a confused look and realizes Jolt is gone. "Well he was there... Oh right I punched the shit out of him. He probably ran off to the restroom or something." Chris laughs while speaking. "Anyway let's go, I'm sure he'll be fine." Amya laughs and questions Chris, "So are we really going to be taking his car?" Chris jumps in the car and sees Jolt left the keys in the car. "Most definitely and besides, he tends to take my car all the time so this is perfect payback." Chris and Amya happily take off with Jolt's car as he is still in the restroom. Whilst Jolt is cleaning up his bloody nose in the bathroom, lights begin to flicker. Jolt looks around with a wet paper towel on his nose wondering why are the lights flickering when there is no storm. He shakes his head as he believes it is nothing to worry about until he hears his name being called by a female voice. "Jolt, Jolt" Small and soothing, but creepy unknown female voice says.

"Hello? Who the fuck just called me? I think I'm going crazy, because…shit I need to get out of here." Jolt attempts to open the bathroom door, but his hand gets burned with a symbol. "Ouch what the fuck?" Jolt screams.

Flickering lights appear to be overshadowing Jolt in the bathroom as he fights to get out. The horror in his soul casts its way out of his body. As he crumbles to the sorrows of death. The end is near for Jolt as he gets snatched by an unknown force in the darkness. His body is pent up against the wall with his face covered in blood. Woman figure with a bunny mask appears walking towards Jolt with grace in her footsteps. "Wha..wha...what are you?" Jolt asks while peeing his pants. The woman reveals her name to be "Jackel Bunny…. And I have come for your soul." Her eyes appear to be pure white as if she is blind, teeth sharp as a wolf and shark. With her nails formed like claws of an ancient beast-like creature. Jackel Bunny grabs Jolt by his throat and begins to feast on his body. Jolt's chest began to hurt severely from the inside out. While clutching his chest in pain, one hand reached for the support of a wall. His hands were clammy and trembling, and he had clinched teeth as sweat dripped from his forehead. At this point, it would presumably only take a straightforward decision to give up or continue, but the decision just didn't seem to come.

His days were like light beer—barely alcoholic and lacking in strength. They were hardly worthwhile investments, which may be why he rarely spent money on them. We yearn to visit and live in the most magnificent settings. How little we are in comparison to them is a measure of their majesty. Amya and Chris are on the road to Rudwick county to have the time of their lives. Listening to popping music and joking around. "I still can't believe I'm actually going to a party right now. I don't ever do this.. Who am I? Haha." Amya feels so alive with Chris in the car as she sticks her hands and head out of the window to feel the air on her face.

Chris smiles ear to ear and tells Amya, "Well I've been trying to tell you to get out sometimes, but no you don't want to listen to me." The best friends both laugh at one another celebrating and are energized like never before. Chris gazes his eyes at Amya admiring her beauty, but believes his love for her is forbidden. He doesn't believe that best friends can't be more than that, at least that is what he tells himself. Chris receives a message on his phone saying, "Are you on the way with the package? Are you still in or are you out?" Chris seems conflicted with whatever motive plan that's going on. "Your phone went off, you want me to answer it for you?" Amya asks concerning Chris. "No! It's fine. It's not important." Chris says nervously, shaking in his skin.

Amya responds, "Are you sure, I don't mind." Chris ignores Amya and just hides his phone in his pocket. Amya becomes very suspicious of Chris and quickly puts her guard up. Back at Amya's dorm where Alyssia is sitting on her bed listening to music on her laptop. A loud uproar began when another student found Jolt's body. The college sirens are gone off and students and professors all run outside to see what could be going on. Alyssia takes off her headphones and notices the loud commotion. "What is going on?" ALyssia questions as she goes to open her dorm room door to investigate while in powerpuff girl pajamas. Unfortunately, her door appears to not want to open as if it's locked from the outside. Alyssia pulls and pulls on the door not noticing the Jackel Bunny is appearing behind her through smoke.  Until Alyssia slowly stops pulling the door and senses an unknown presence behind her. She slowly turns around and recognizes the Jackel Bunny. Alyssia fears for her life when her face is filled with tears as she pleads for her life. "Wait now this wasn't the deal. I was told if  I sent her to that house, I would be spared. Please don't do this." The Jackel Bunny walks intensively to Alyssia and pushes her against the door and laughs with evil intentions. Jackel Bunny licks Alyssia's face with her ten inch tongue and tastes the sin on her. "Indeed you have done that task correctly, but I know your dirty secret and your sin is tasty." Alyssia is confused by what Jackel Bunny could be talking about. "What are you talking about?"

Secrets could be the death of

you.

# Chapter 5

These are the Seven Social Sins:

Affluence without labor.

Pleasure that is sinless.

Knowledge devoid of personality.

Without morality, commerce

Without humanity, science

Worship with no offering.

Politics devoid of morals.

The forbidden has a fascination that renders it

unspeakable. Unquestionably, the most harmful vice,

if you will, a person can have. Self pity is considered

a greater evil than pride, which is considered the

first of the seven deadly sins. The worst feeling

anyone can have is self-pity. And the most harmful.

Where am I? Oh. I remain here. Alone. Forgotten. I'm still losing blood, and I wish it would stop. I want it to finish immediately; please let it do so.

Please let this end already. I'm worn out. I am dying, I am sure of it. I'm waiting to die while lying in my own blood. Will it please just finish.

I must be able to accomplish something. Anything. I must live because I wish to. Please, I can't go out like this. How am I going to escape this mess? There has to be a way out of this situation. I could remain here for hours since it's so calm. I don't have a choice right now, though. I do have a choice, though. I have the option of giving up or fighting. I'm leaving this place as soon as I can and won't return until I've located assistance. I need assistance to leave this place. It is useless for me to attempt it alone. I know I'm going

to pass away. I am aware that it is now too late to
save me. Alright, come grab me death. I no longer
feel terrified. Please move quickly; I don't have
endless amounts of time.  I am unable to make sense
of everything because of the fog. Although my head
is too heavy to lift, I feel dizzy. The paradox: The time
is not now. I had to close my eyes because I can't
handle this. The devastation of Alyssia has come as
Jackel Bunny rips into her body with sharp fangs and
nails. Alyssia's blood splats all over the room as she
attempts to run away, but the grip of Jackel Bunny
was too strong to bear. Screaming and crawling as
she tried, but was snatched and ripped into parts.
Her soul has now become a part of Jackel Bunny.
Alyssia was kind, opportunistic, upbeat, and
sometimes a touch too naive. However, what would

you anticipate from someone in her position? She was born at an important port to a typical family. Up until she was approximately 15 years old, she had a trouble-free life; after that, things started to change. She held a significant position and was rising in popularity. She had overcome many challenges and was now, in a quick world, learning hidden truths. But nothing could stop her from making the world a better place with her charm and abilities. She had the potential to inspire many people immediately. After a long ride of silence within the car Chris and Amya arrive at the house where the party takes place. The house is the same place where Tanner was brought to from Sabrina Jackel. Everything looks so dark and abandoned which makes Amya worried about this so-called party. "Where is everyone? Why does it seem so deserted here?" Amya asks as she looks at Chris concerned for her life. "Chris! Why aren't you talking to me? Say something." Amya continued to raise her voice to get answers from Chris. Chris with teary eyes says, "I'm sorry for this, but I have no choice." He quickly grabs her and gives a shot in her neck to make her fall asleep. Sabrina Jackel approaches as Amya is falling to deep sleep and kisses Chris and says to him, "You did a great job… you shall be rewarded." Chris seems to be regretful and says, "I'll do whatever to stay alive… you got him inside." Sabrina smiles with greed to tell Chris, "Yeah you were right about this Tanner boy. He really is easy to catch, especially being such a hormonal kid. Let's go and bring her inside for the celebration. It's almost time to feast."

The beautiful art of magic is to astonish your

audience to the point where nothing else does. Any

impossibility becomes a reality. Creation draws

something out of the void. Startups take something

and give it—possibly at first for free—to others who

are unaware. Not the insider tricks or the actual

secret codes, but the illusion of magic and the

enchantment of illusion are what we are most

interested in. We look for the confusion, the

inconsistencies, the amusements, and the countless

emotions that uncomfortably vibrate through the

crowd. Not knowledge but mystery and deception are

what we seek. We desire to look at the impossibility.

We crave astonishment and surprises. We are seeking

for a real story, but one that is too complex to fully

convey. We will have found magic once we learn

about that tale. The voice was resonant with a million midnights, with darkness and stars tied for all time in a single, impenetrable bundle.

Police are swarmed at the sighting of the deaths of Jolt and Alyssia. "What happened here? How are these two people connected? Especially since the place of their deaths are so close to each other on this campus." The captain of the police department asks as she investigates both crime scenes. Captain Murphy looks around the bathroom and is disgusted by how Joly's body looks drained as if all his blood was sucked out his body. "Nothing, but bone and skin is here. Is it the same with the girl in her dorm room?" Captain Murphy asks the detective. Detective Macauley explains what he has seen from Alyssia, "I just found that this girl's name is Alyssia and her roommate who is also her cousin is Amya Fitzgerald." He shows Captain Murphy a picture of Alyssia and Amya. "They are both beautiful young women. I don't believe she could be a suspect, because this seems too non-human to do." Captain Murphy contemplates. A bony, melancholy face is covered partially by ginger, shoulder-length hair. Asymmetrically positioned, pitiful hazel eyes look longingly over the ones they have protected for so long. His bad luck in battles is still being punished by a gunshot wound that extends from the top of his left face down to the left side of his lips and ends on his chin. This is the image of Detective Macauley Valkeiki, one of several lucky officers. Despite his rugged build, he stands respectfully amid others.

A nice, endearing face is just visible beneath ginger brown, long hair. Glistening emerald eyes that are gracefully positioned within their sockets look lovingly over the nation they have grown to love for such a long time.

Her fair skin perfectly complements her brown eyes and hair, leaving a pleasing impression of her good looks. Captain Jessica Murphy, a real visionary and leader among the officers. She has an alluring quality, which can be her hatred or just her general demeanor.

A snarl in the mist, a crash of earth, and all of a sudden you are faced with a massive soul of flesh and disease. Another roar comes from its disordered mouth with deafening ferocity, and two vicious eyes gaze at you with a terrible obsession.  Its skeletal head, which is faceless, is covered in shadowy hair.

The creature's forked nostrils, nestled inside a

shriveled nose, breathe calmly. Its tiny, stringy body

is above a bony head. Who knows what the backstory

is, but every square inch of it is covered in

otherworldly armor.

It advances slowly, its six legs carrying its

condemned body with a gloomy vigor. The snap of a

whip can be heard with each of its quick motions,

and a vine-like tail wriggles behind it. Two flimsy

wings spread out completely. Spiky bones and

incorporeal feathers extend skyward as though

attempting to fully obstruct you. Unimpressed eyes

nevertheless cast a fleeting glance your way. The

demon Corpse Fiend has come to the surface and

meets up with the Jackel Bunny in a cemetery of

Rudwick County. "Master, you have arrived earlier than expected." Jackal Bunny speaks as she kneels before the Corpse fiend. "The feast is about to begin, my precious soul. You have done well and now your counterpart Sabrina will do hers." Corpse Fiend says to Jackel Bunny as he praises her. Jackel Bunny with all her humble might to the corpse fiend asks, "What shall you have me do now master?" Smiling with gratitude and deceit the corpse fiend tells Jackel Bunny, "return to sabrina and reunite as one and let the fun games begin."

# Chapter 6

I, Sabrina Jackel, had to fight my entire life, and people know that I'm rude, unbiased, and fearless. But people don't realize that someone with my bad past has more than this. I was born and raised in a prosperous family in a dysfunctional neighborhood. Up until I was around 8 years old, I had a peaceful life, but then things started to change. I became a member of a dark clan after maiming someone during a protracted heatwave. I had to make it through a chaotic environment with a couple of companions. But with my cleverness and bravery, I was able to overcome my doubts and worries as well as the forces of nature. I became the woman I am now because of this. The only flip side of things is that I am way older than people would believe. I'm

not an average twenty or thirty something year old

woman. My life spans over a century as I have been

reborn. I was born in 1815 to a mother and father

who didn't really want me in the first place. They

went by the name of Howard and Melinda Asher. You

may be wondering where I got my name Jackel from,

we will get to that revelation shortly. You see, Syfer

Keep wasn't always its name. Its original name used

to be Jackel Horde Mississippi. I got my name Jackel

from the original name of my home town.

Everything changed over the years when my family

and others were accused of witchcraft. My family had

abilities, but we weren't evil. I tried to be the good

daughter to explain to people that we may have

powers, but they are not evil. As far as I knew my

deadbeat father gave me up as a sacrifice to the leaders of the land and said I was the witch in the family. He spreaded allegations of me practicing dark magic secretly when one night he saw my hands with fire flowing out. That night he saw me, I discovered my power, but didn't understand it. I screamed for help, but he automatically called me a witch and had me murdered by hanging me on a tree. My mother had the power of healing and my father had the power of mind manipulation. He literally could make people believe things that are not true. I don't know how involved my mother was in the process of my death, but I cared not. I died and went to the burning fires of hell and made a deal with a demon prince, Corpse Fiend. My time in hell wasn't always unpleasurable. I made many friends like a demon named Frank and another soul named Carl. I was able to get really close to a woman down there who has a similar story as me. Her name is Ogmedassi and you will learn about her story another time. I would say that I never wanted to be a dark or evil being, but I would be lying. I always knew deep down I was sadistic when I fantasized about the inside of people's bodies. I wondered how our liver would taste outside the body, I bet it tasted raw like sushi. It could be slimy, but satisfying and delicious. Just thinking about it makes my bloody mouth water. Nice words and a decent appearance don't necessarily mean that a person is nice; in my opinion, the nicer you look, the more dishonest you come across as being. The status of facts and evidence cannot be changed by our intentions, preferences, or the dictates of our feelings because facts are obstinate objects. Over time as I came back from hell living on this earth, I've killed so many souls and it was divine. It was a choice I didn't hesitate to make, especially since I'm already condemned to hell in the first place. My deal with the Corpse Fiend was to spread havoc and bring him souls to torture for all eternity. My first task I actually begged for was getting vengeance on my parents. The corpse fiend has a fetish of spreading let's just say bad mental health problems around to people. He taught me how to discover my own powers, which I learned how to duplicate my own alter ego, "The Jackel Bunny."

The Jackel Bunny didn't come until about just in the past two years. She was born in 2020, so yeah I got my own hands dirty for centuries. 2020 was the year I failed to get a certain soul and literally died in a car accident wearing a bunny mask and dress. I was heading to the place where that soul was the corpse fiend wanted so badly. Until I got crushed and pushed off the road down a rocky cliff. My punishment for not getting that soul was that I had to spend two years in a cage in hell. Now it's halloween 2022 I had to catch up on soul snatching. It was double the fun when Jackel Bunny got the ones I couldn't get myself without getting caught. Since this world is so filled and backed up with technology, I would have gotten taken again.

# Chapter 7

Halloween is such a beautiful deadly holiday and perfect time to kill. Now it's time to feast as my alter ego, Jackel Bunny, has been sent back to recontinue with me. It's time to feast and party.

I already know karma is going to bite me in the ass someday for doing this Amya and Tanner. I knew deep down I shouldn't have accepted the deal, but I needed the help. My life was a living shit show and I was desperate. Hopefully I can make things right, but it's more than likely too late, because what's about to happen. "Sabrina! Where are you at? I got everyone ready downstairs now." I asked as I walked in on her merging with a demon. "What the fuck is this?" Sabrina looks back at me and explains,

"Chris... My poor Chris, everything is fine." I couldn't understand what was going on, so I freaked out and said, "I just saw you sucking or merging up a demon. Whatever that was."

She laughs with blood in her mouth and says to me, "Oh! Yeah that's right you don't know about my powers. Yeah that's my alter ego Jackel Bunny. She was sent back by our boss, so we can get this ritual done." Sabrina and her demon horde thing walks aways and leaves me with more regret for doing all of this. Before I got myself into this situation, I began to travel frequently and was meeting some wonderful new people. I was attempting to rise to the top in a fantastic world with a wonderful companion. But nothing can stop me from realizing my full potential because of my courage and honesty. I might soon grow into an unstoppable force. I'm still figuring out where I belong in the world, though. I believe there is yet more to discover about this globe. Fortunately, I have a lot of resources to help him. I, at least, think so.  We all gather downstairs in the living room with Amya and Tanner both tied up in chairs. I became really shocked when an old friend who I didn't know was here had joined this freak show as well. "What a minute? You are a part of this too?" My friend Malacki laughs and says, "Bro I have been a part of this longer than you buddy." A young, weathered face is just slightly hidden by long, ginger hair. The place they have spent so much time seeking refuge in is watched over by heavy brown eyes that are nicely set inside their sockets. His cheekbones and eyes are gracefully complemented by his soft skin, leaving a pleasing reminder of his good fortune.

That's cocky Malacki for ya, used to be one of my

brothers from high school. I haven't seen him in

years. "What do you mean you've been a part of

this?" I shouldn't have trusted this in the first place,

because there is so much more I didn't even know.

"Well I see you boys have met, come on the games

are about to begin. They are waking up now."

Sabrina says.

Malacki looks at me and walks away and I grab his

arm and tell him we are not done talking about this.

"Oh, but we are. As a matter of fact, you are about to

hear my story in a minute buddy." Sadistic smile lays

on his face as he stands beside Sabrina.

Like finger painters in first-grade art class, they

experimented with black magic, and the majority of

them either perished as a result of their works or fled the nightmares they wreaked. Whatever they are about to do to my friends I can't sit back and watch this. Amya I'm sorry, but I have to go. I walked away to the front door, but was stopped by Sabrina's power. "Where do you think you are going Chris? There is no way to back out of this now. You made a blood oath, remember? If you try and live your soul will forever be the corpse fiend." I was stunned and wondered what the hell she was talking about. "Who the fuck is the corpse fiend, I made no such deal to whatever this thing you speak of." Sabrina's head tilts sideways and smiles deeply and says, "Oh, but you definitely did." I didn't buy her bluff, so I attempted to leave and got caught up. Her Jackel Bunny alter ego came after me as I was walking out the door. I was struck directly in my chest by a blade, but the blade was her hand. The Jackel Bunny shapeshifted her hand into an exquisite deep orange stingray leather grip holding a fairly broad, wide, jagged blade fashioned of obsidian. This weapon's fine, sharp edge makes it perfect for piercing adversaries and turning them into sieves. A jagged, slightly curved crossguard on the blade hand adds weight to the blade for better weight balance and provides hand protection in combat. Increasing amounts of blood. Why won't it stop if it simply keeps leaking out? I'm standing in a pool of my own blood, and it just keeps gushing and flowing. My strength is dwindling by the minute and I've already knelt down. Considering how weary I already am, perhaps I should get some rest. Get my body moving.

Please, just collapse. No way out is available. Oh my God, I'm going to die right now. I want to live, so please say no. I mustn't, I can't, die. Please lend a hand to me, anyone. I'd rather not pass away. I'd rather not pass away. Why would I even beg to help when no one is available to do so. My last hope is for Amya and Tanner to survive this horror. I should have told her how I felt from the beginning, but now it will never happen. My love for her will continue, but my body and soul will pass. But wait, I'm not going without taking someone with me. They didn't noticed I secretly attached a bomb within Malacki's jacket when I grabbed him. I knew something was up from the beginning, but I couldn't let anyone think I was smart. They thought I was playing their game, but in reality I had my own plan in place.

What they  didn't see is that the rope that Tanner and Amya are tied in is actually cut. They are pretending to be knocked out, because when Sabrina had me tie them up I whispered in their ears about my plan. Of course, I had to apologize to both of them for getting them into this. All of this was in motion before I walked upstairs to get Sabrina. Malacki was a bonus, because I really didn't know he was here. Luckily for me he is still a dumbass and was the best target to place my small bomb. "Well before I die, Malacki, I typically remember that you love explosives." I said as I was grabbing my last smoke and my phone where my bomb is linked to. Malacki with a confused look stares at me and says, "Dude, you are dying and you want to talk about explosives… just die already." Sabrina seems concerned and is curious about what I could be speaking about. "Oh I'm about to die alright, but I'm not going alone. See you in hell buddy. Amya! Tanner! Run! Now! Run!!" Tanner and Amya both woke up and punched Sabrina and Malacki in the face. As soon as I saw them run out the door I made the house explode with Malacki's body.

Her elegant garment has a draped neckline and drapes from top to bottom, subtly revealing the traditional dress underneath. Her dress' soft, tightly-knotted fabric covers her stomach, where a sizable cloth band worn high around her waist breaks up the continuous flow. The dress unzips to expose the dress underneath beneath the fabric band. The upper dress has a much shorter front that curves outward, while the back flows behind her for a brief distance before ending in a wide rectangle.

The same fabric and color used to outline the bottom

and neckline of the dress are also utilized to divide

her relatively short and wide arms into smaller,

delicate bands below the shoulder.The same fabric

and color used to outline the bottom and neckline of

the dress are also utilized to divide her relatively

short and wide arms into smaller, delicate bands

below the shoulder. I can't believe it's been two

months now, since Chris sacrificed himself to save

Tanner and I.

# Chapter 8

It was hard coming back to college after everything happened, especially finding out about Alyssia and Jolt. This dress I'm wearing represents my cousin Alyssia, because she was supposed to wear this dress for the upcoming college play. This play is being produced by some movie studio in florida called DBSfilms. I never knew who they were, but from what I heard is they have an amazing talented community. I thought I would be passed it all with the Sabrina Jackel thing, but something still feels off. Especially doing my time in that house she had me and Tanner trapped in. Before I knew Tanner was there Sabrina kept her mouth going on and on and I remember her saying something about Alyssia secret sins. What could have Alyssia done so bad that led her to be a victim. Well besides her making a deal with a demon in the first place, we all know that was stupid. Demons don't keep their word literally all the time, but there was something more going on with Alyssia that I have to figure out. In the meantime, I am going to work my tail off for this play and I'm so happy they are dedicating it to Alyssia. Get to where others are expecting you to be, then keep going. Wherever people anticipated me to end up, I've always attempted to take an extra step. You must do something even if you don't think you can. You must take on challenges you perceive as impossible. "It's almost showtime, you ready for this Amya." Tanner asked me backstage as he is dressed as a tree character. "Oh my god! What are you wearing? Wait, what character are you? You look good tho Tan the man... well tree.”

Tanner and I have become close for the past two months, since leaving Rudwick County. We both laugh at each other with excitement. Tanner says, “I’m just a random tree by standard I guess you call it, but I’m not really a character. I just really wanted to be a tree and it works for me tho. You look beautiful tho and I’m sure Alyssia would be truly proud of you.” It’s time for me to go on stage and I was so excited, but something happened that shocked everyone. Once I got on stage, I suddenly became really dizzy and I couldn’t see. With my head rolling in circles, my eyes getting blurry, I saw a glimpse of a demon face in the crowd as I fell to the ground. Next thing I know, I wake up in an abandoned cabin in the woods with the number 13 on it. It feels like I'm in some sort of a dream world, but it's like a forest in the dark. The forest was large, dark, and old-fashioned. Redwood, hazel, and sycamore shaded their canopy, and enough sparkling light peaked through their crowns for a number of sprouts to appear in the rich, nutrient-rich soils below. Most trees had swaying climbing plants hanging from them, and a variety of flowers that flourished in profusion brought color to the otherwise lifeless terrain. The forest was alive with a variety of horrible noises, most of which were made by little animals and were not in time with the wind's rustling of the leaves or the branches of the treetops. I don't know where I could be or if anyone can hear me. "What is wrong with her? Will she be ok?" Tanner is at the hospital asking doctors questions about Amya's condition. The doctor's couldn't give an explanation about her condition to Tanner, because they don't know what could be going on. In the meantime Tanner goes and gets snacks and is approached by Captain Murphy and Detective Macauley. Tanner, sitting on the bed side of Amya, is approached by Captain Murphy and Detective Macauley. "Your name is Tanner right?" Captain Murphy asks. "Yes ma'am, that's me. What is this about? We spoke to you guys two months ago about our situation. I hope everything is solved by now." Tanner speaks while worrying about Amya. Detective responds, "Well for the past two months son, I know it's been rough. Especially surviving a burning house, but I remember you said there was a girl and another guy who trapped you guys correct?" Tanner says, "Yeah, she went by the name Sabrina Jackel, why are we bringing this back up again?" Captain Murphy and Detective look at each other concerned and confused. "Why are you guys looking at each other as if I'm crazy or something?" Captain Murphy explains to Tanner, "Well for the past two months we have been investigating everything. One we only found two bodies, your friend Chris and the other guy Malacki fellow. There was no other body besides them and this Sabrina Jackel you speak of… this name goes back centuries ago to a young witch who is dead." Murphy continues, "Either this girl went by a fake name or something else happened." Tanner replies, "Something else like what? Please tell me what could have happened? Oh yeah you can't, because you weren't there now were you." Tanner wishes for Murphy and Macauley to leave him alone and they respect his wishes, but they left their card with him. It's crucial to keep asking questions. Curiosity has its own purpose in life. When one considers the wonders of eternity, life, and the amazing design of reality, one cannot help but be in awe. Even making a small effort each day to understand a bit more of this mystery is sufficient. The mystery is the most wonderful experience we can have. True art and true science have their roots in this primordial emotion. The sense of mystery and wonder is not destroyed by knowledge. More mystery is constantly present. There are many obvious things in the world that, for some reason, no one ever notices. The tonic of wildness is what we need. While

we are genuinely interested in discovering and
learning about everything, we also demand that
everything be mysterious and unknowable. We
demand that the land and the sea remain uncharted,
unexplored, and unfathomable for as long as
possible. There is never enough of the natural world.
Nothing develops an undeveloped mind's capacities
more than a trail leading off into the night; nothing
stimulates the intellect more than a strong suspicion.
Many things that escape persons who only dream at
night are known to those who dream during the day.
They see glimpses of eternity in their drab visions,
and when they awaken, they are thrilled to learn
that they were just about to discover the big secret.
They pick up bits of knowledge about excellent
wisdom and more about the knowledge that is

simply bad. An inner tranquility that radiates is elegance. Grace is the capacity to give, accept, and be grateful. Mystery is a secret chuckle that is always ready to come out! Glamor is like the moon; it only glows when the sun is shining; it only radiates if there is supreme daring and bravery within. Within the dreamworld, where Amya lies. It's like you proceed through the ominous doorway that is tucked away among the trees. You're greeted with a demanding world right away. Beyond a few yards, a dense fog hovers in the air, obstructing your eyesight. You are at liberty to investigate what resides in the river, what is concealed in the cave, or where the forest stops. Because of these awful circumstances, you feel exposed and in danger.

Without a doubt, this world is dangerous, but for the time being, you should be able to handle it.

You sense the air vibrations of creatures you previously believed only lived in people's dreams in the distant distance. You strive to stay away from them even if they don't seem troubled by your presence. There are clearly flying creatures, hairy creatures, and what appear to be creatures with muscles of some type. Even the most beautiful of things can be turned into a nightmare of terror. The dreamworld preys on your fantasy, just to turn it into a terrifying nightmare. Weapons, blood, and devastation are all throughout the woodland. What was once a peaceful, rich woodland is now the scene of a brutal conflict, and its new colors are red, silver, and khaki.

A sight straight out of nightmares, the air, which would ordinarily be delicate and quiet, is suddenly flaming red with fire and dense with smoke, ash, and embers. Both the environment and humanity have suffered greatly as a result. It will probably take a very long time for this woodland to recover. It's obvious that the plants, grass, and shrubs have been replaced by blood, bodies, and rubbish. The wounded of one side are lying in vast groupings throughout the woodland, but the combatants' faces are full of optimism, and they are pressing the enemy with increasing force. Amya runs as fast as she could, but each time she does she only goes deeper into the hole of deception. Evil laughs of Sabrina Jackel are heard as echoes throughout the dreamworld as Amya hastily runs for her life. Knowing it could be her last

time alive, she continues to fight to get back home.

# Chapter 9

What was once a dress is now nothing more than a dreadful old piece of fabric full of holes and smeared with grime, it just manages to hang from her shoulders like an abandoned old towel.

Much of her is exposed to the outdoors due to a significant tear on the right side. She is dressed, with an old coat over it. Even if it just partially shields her from the wind, it's still a ragged, filthy, smelling mess. Her clothes are also in bad condition. The right leg is covered with tiny tears, while the left leg has a large tear that has split it in half. She does, however, have shoes to keep her feet safe. The sole of the left shoe has come away at the heel, and they are only the appropriate size and lack laces. She has a huge scarf wrapped around her face and around her neck, covering her chin. Despite having several holes, it is still holding together. Surprisingly, the bandana that covers her head doesn't have any holes, stains, or other significant faults outside its age.

It's so dark in here and I don't know what I am sitting on. It feels as if I am strapped to a seat or something and a bowl-like thing is attached to my head. Wait, I can hear footsteps coming from a distance. I can wiggle my arms as they feel strapped down to a chair. A light starts to beam through the dark as I can see someone. I can't see their whole body just yet, but I can sense it could be a person.

"Amya can you hear us sweetie? Squeeze my hand if you can hear us?" A woman's voice I could hear, but I didn't know how to respond. My body is stiff and I can't move. Hand clapping I hear in this shadowy

hell and the noise is getting closer. "Sweet Sweet

Amya.. you thought that was a way out." Oh no! It's

Sabrina Jackel again, haven't seen her in over two

months. How is this even possible? "Sabrina? How

the fuck are you alive? Where am I?" I asked while

realizing she had me trapped in an electric chair in a

dark room of some sort. "Amya... Amya poor girl,

you really thought that explosion stopped anything.

It was all according to plan. You see my deal with the

corpse fiend he shows me things before they happen.

Oh wait you don't know who that is... well long story

short he is a demon prince lord of Hell that brings

me back." Sabrina appears in a dress as she speaks to

me. Only one of her shoulders is covered by the dress,

leaving the other exposed as it falls into a

straightforward v-neck. The dress looks comfy, yet elegant and attractive thanks to the loose fit.

Just above her elbows, her arms have been completely covered. The sleeves are understated yet stylish. a flawless marriage of grace and sophistication. The waist of the dress is slim, but it's a close fit. Her waist is made more visible but not overly so by a modest, exquisite belt.

The dress becomes wider and more sundress-like below the waist. Just above her ankles, the dress is a little longer on the sides. Scarpins, the ideal accessory for this outfit, are on her. She also had on a tiny, sophisticated cap and an embroidered bracelet to finish it all off. "Why are you wearing a dress?" I asked. "Oh! Just because I think this is really fun and cute. This dress was actually your cousin's Alyssia.

She was going to give it to you, but she died before that could happen. WHOOPS!" Sabrina continues to torture me as I feel my life force being drained away from me. "Why did you have to kill her? What did she do?" Sabrina explains, "OH WoW! Alyssia didn't tell you about her past. Welp... she wasn't as innocent as she played off to be. Have you heard about the young guy who was said to have drowned in his bathtub at the age of 15. News flash his cause of death wasn't truly drowning. He was brutally murdered by Alyssia when she sliced his neck and stabbed him over 200 times. She was a secret babysitter killer that no one knew about. She went on a spree of kills soon after and murdered other innocent teenagers. She loved the thrill of it after being inspired by the movie Halloween. You know?

The Michael Myers guy movie. I'm sure I actually met her victims before. Hmmm.. what were their names??? Ah! Yes, Evan Berry, Kesha, Harrison, J'beck, and others. The Corpse Fiend was thrilled about her." I wanted to be angry in disbelief, but my energy was draining rapidly. "But why me? I saw you at my campus dressed in a bloody rabbit mask and short dress. What makes me so special?" Sabrina walks to me and lifts my chin up with her wolf sharp like nails. She looks at me with her deadly white eyes and deformed skin. She says to me, "We need a virgin in order for my red skinned friend here to enter the earth. He's been a sleep demon for a long time. Meaning he travels around people's minds to kill them in their sleep. Even though deep down he doesn't want to do that, he is so damn good at it."

Sabrina continues, "You are the pure virgin soul I was sent to get a few years back when I saw you at that party, but now I got you." You suddenly find yourself face to face with a towering figure of heat and blood after hearing a groan in the nebula and seeing a bolt of lightning. As it trades glances with you, its gaping mouth lets out another loud moan and its six flaming eyes stare at you with a dazed violence. Its oval head, which itself appears to be shifting continually, is covered with a thick head of hair. The creature has stumpy nostrils that are forked and emit toxic fog.  Its enormous, inflated torso is atop an oval-shaped head. Although its skin shows signs of electric powers, you don't want to learn the likely horrible details. The creature moves closer to you, its four legs carrying its enormous body with ease and a restless intensity. Electric

energies pulse from a vine-like tail that spins behind

it with each motion. The thing hasn't stopped staring

at you, and you haven't been able to turn away.

# Chapter 10

Amya clenched her eyes tight out of fear. She was certain that whatever was causing the excruciatingly intense aches in her leg wouldn't be attractive. Her body as a whole urged her to halt what she was doing, pause, and find some relief from this agonizing sensation. Multiple voices kept repeating in her head. Some predict she will be alright, while others predict she won't. She let out a groaning yelp that was equal parts desperate and determined. She could either fight or give up. But today, she was either unable or unwilling to deal with the grief. The biting and clawing of the demon is visibly shown in the real world as she lays in the hospital. Tanner shouts for help to the doctors as Amya's body bounces as if she is having a seizure. Blood and white foam looking mess pours out her mouth as in the dream world she is fighting the demon creature. Blood runs down my body, through my clothing, and onto the ground. It's warm, and it has a pleasant feeling. But it shouldn't; I must be dying because this is the end of me.

But I'm still standing; I'm not moving. Despite my legs' pleading, I refuse to let go and sink to the lush grass below. My legs no longer feel anything. It's beginning to feel numb everywhere. Perhaps it would be best if I lay down. I need to conserve my energy because this is a waste. I'm confident that if I lay down, I will survive this and live. I'll just lay down for the time being because someone will find me shortly. The demon has stopped for now and I don't know if he will be back. My soul is damaged and forsaken, I don't think God can save me or even want to save me. Maybe my time has come to die, but I hope tanner is fine and healthy. My time on this earth wasn't meant to be long like others. Sabrina approaches my body as I fade away into the afterlife. Her eyes are bloody red and her teeth are sharp as swords. Her voice has gotten deep as she transcends into something more fierce than ever. Sabrina grasps her hand through my bloody body and launches her nine foot tongue out to lick my blood off her hands. As my last breath is taken I feel my soul is taken. I can't take too much longer, my life can go on no longer. Goodbye everyone….. The closer you look…the less you will see.

"AHHHHH!!" Amya awakens with a loud scream back in the cabin where it is foreseen. "Wait what the fuck is this? I saw all of you die and I saw myself die. How am I in this chair and back in this cabin again? Chris died blowing everything up by putting a small bomb in Malacki's jacket pocket." Sabrina, Chris, Malacki all look at the deranged Amya and laugh hysterically at her rant. "Damn dude, what the fuck did you put in that knock out juice." Malacki laughs and asks Chris. Chris laughs and says, "Well apparently it was strong enough to make her see some weird shit."

Sabrina Jackel looks into Amya eyes and say, "You had one hell of a ride didn't you sweetie. Yeah I have more power than you think. I made you see your desires and made you believe it was real. Chris doesn't love you like that and he certainly knows

what he is doing. You see we all here made a deal

with the Corpse Fiend demon to sacrifice virgins in

his name to bring him glory. Also to let us live for all

eternity, so we won't have to be in that hell hole.

LITERALLY."

Sabrina reveals to Amya that those Detectives she

thought she saw were actually not real either. "Yeah

those Detective Macauley and Captain Murphy people

you saw, they weren't real police either. How about I

introduce you to the murphy slain killers. Jessica and

Macauley Murphy, brother and sister duo who are

notorious serial killers."

They act impulsively and with fierceness. However,

someone with a history of murder has more to offer

than this. They were raised in a small family in a

typical port where they were born and raised. Up until they were about 11 years old, everything was peaceful. They were dark in their hearts as a result of their parents' cruelty. Due to a freak fire that destroyed their home, they were forced to leave and were alone. They had to survive on a harsh planet with a pet. But they overcame all obstacles with tenacity and cunning to become the best killers there are and stay one step ahead of the game.

They became the murderers they are today as a result of this.

# Chapter 11

A ritual is a myth brought to life. Additionally, you participate in the narrative by performing the rite. You are, in a sense, being put in accord with that wisdom, which is the wisdom that is inherent within you regardless, by engaging in a ritual or participating in the myth because myth is a projection of the depth of wisdom of the psyche. Your own life's wisdom is being brought to the forefront of your consciousness. The capacity to deal with suffering may be our minds' greatest talent. The four doors of the mind, which each person passes through in accordance with their needs, are a concept from classical philosophy. The entrance to sleep is first. We can escape the outside world and all its suffering by sleeping. As time passes, sleep helps us put the things that have hurt us in the past behind us. When someone gets hurt, they frequently lose consciousness. Similar to how when hearing distressing news, people frequently swoon or faint. The mind has entered the first door as a means of defending itself against pain. Secondly, there is the door of forgetfulness. There are some wounds that cannot or will not heal completely. There is also no way to heal from certain memories because they are just awful. All wounds do not heal with time, as the proverb claims. Most wounds heal with time. Behind this door, the rest are concealed. The gateway to madness comes in third. When the mind suffers a severe blow, it can occasionally retreat into madness. Although it might not seem like it, this is useful.

There are moments when reality is nothing but pain,
and the mind must turn away from reality in order
to stop the pain. The gateway to death comes last. the
last option. We have been informed that once we are
dead, nothing can harm us. The human race is a
boring endeavor. The majority of people spend the
majority of their time working in order to survive,
and what little freedom they do have makes them so
fearful that they will use any and all means at their
disposal to avoid it.  This form of crazy involves a
certain kind of suffering, joy, loneliness, and dread.
When you're wasted, it's amazing. Like shooting
stars, the thoughts and emotions come to you
quickly and frequently. You follow them until you
find better, brighter ones. Shyness fades, the correct
movements and words appear out of nowhere, and

the ability to capture people becomes a felt certainty.
Even uninteresting individuals have interests.
Sensuality is everywhere, and both the urge to
seduce others and to be seduced are insatiable. One's
marrow is filled with feelings of comfort, intensity,
power, well-being, financial omnipotence, and
ecstasy. But this alters someplace. There are far too
many and the rapid ideas are moving too quickly;
clarity is being replaced by overwhelming confusion.
Memories fade. Fear and worry have taken the place
of friends' amusement and concentration.
Everything that was once going your way is suddenly
going against it; you are agitated, furious, terrified,
unmanageable, and completely immersed in the
mental darkness. You were unaware that the caves

even existed. Because crazy creates its own reality, it will never cease.

"Are we ready to begin the ritual for the feast of the beast?" Sabrina Jackel speaks to her cult. Everyone says, "Yes we are." The ritual sayings begins with, "Some fangs, shining moist from black dog gums, yearn to rip. You do not open your eyes at the conclusion. Such a mouth shouldn't be observed up close. The speckled lips will curl back in a whinny of anticipation prior to the bite, before it's forgetfulness in the goring of your tender bits. You can just feel it." Continues with, "This ebony bird then tricked my melancholy imagination into laughing thanks to its severe and dignified demeanor.

Tell me what your lordly name is on the Night's Plutonian shore even if your crest is shorn and shaven, ghastly gloomy, and aged raven roaming from the Nightly shore. Let the blood of the virgin soothe your thirst, for we call upon the ancient demon of hell to feast on the corpus shell." The house shakes as if the earth is quaking. Sabrina and her cult are consumed with power or darkness as their bodies transform into creatures of hell. Loud thunder and lightning roams the dark skies as evil gates of hell open to the realm of earth. Amya struggles to get out of the chair and falls back. As soon as she falls back she turns and notices Tanner is long gone with his face smashed in by the staircase of the cabin house.

# Chapter 12

Sabrina Jackel Bunny is merged into one demon-like bastard from hell. The creature has elegantly placed bright crimson eyes within a scaled, angular cranium that gives it a menacing aspect. On top of its head, right above its diminutive, cat-like ears, is one small center horn. Each of its jaw lines has a series of tiny horns running down the sides.

It has a short horn on its chin, a sharp snout, and two tiny, pointed nostrils. Its mouth has a few noticeable teeth that protrude from the side and hint at the fear that lies within. Its head is followed by a broad neck that descends into a massive body. The top has smooth skin, and its spine is adorned with a row of spikes.

Its bottom is significantly paler in color than the rest of its body and covered in reptile skin. The creature can stand sturdily and haughtily because of its six thin limbs, which carry its body. Each leg has five digits that terminate in powerful talons that appear to be composed of crystal. Its shoulders give way to obscene wings that extend to the bottom of its back. The wings are bat-like, with several tiny holes on their inner sides, and each bone's end sprouts a pair of sharp hooks. Its graceful tail has the same silky skin as its body and a fan-like tip at the end. Chris transitions into the creature with long, narrow eyes made of onyx that are hidden inside its long, narrow skull, giving it a terrifying aspect. Over its thick, spherical ears, on top of its head, are several massive center horns. Each of its jaw lines is covered in several rows of tiny tendrils.

Its chin is covered in tiny crystal growths, and its round nose has two tiny, pointed nostrils. Rows of enormous teeth protrude from the side of its mouth, yet they merely hint at the fear that is concealed inside. From its head, a lengthy neck extends into a long body. Rows of tendrils run along its spine, and the top has thick skin covering it. Curved scales cover its underside, which is significantly lighter in color than the rest of its body. Its body is supported by four enormous limbs, which also allow it to stand imposingly tall. Each of the six digits on each limb has thorny talons that resemble onyx at the end. The delicate wings extend all the way down to the animal's pelvis, starting just below its shoulders.

The top of each visible bone is covered in sharp, spiky scales, and the wings have a triangular shape. The inner sides of the wings are also filled with small holes. It has the same thick skin as its body and a thick tail that terminates in a hammer-like development. Lights flashing through the darkness as Amya appears to free herself as the chair breaks from her fall. She runs out the front door as the others continue to transition. Malacki could be the ugliest of them all. The creature has broad, hard eyes made of onyx that sit narrowly within its hard, narrow skull, giving it a threatening aspect.

On top of its head, right above its tiny, curled ears, are many tendrils. Each of its jaw lines is flanked by a broad fan-like structure of skin and bone.

Its chin is covered with tiny horns, and its long nose

has two wide, rounded nostrils. A few pointed teeth

protrude from the side of its mouth, revealing the

dread that is concealed within. Its head is followed by

a long, slender neck and body. Its spine is lined with

rows of heavy armor plate, and the top is coated with

scales that resemble stones.

Its bottom is much darker in color than the rest of its

body and is covered in silky skin. The creature can

stand erect and towering thanks to two enormous

limbs carrying its body. Each leg has five digits that

culminate in slender talons that appear to be formed

of stone. Huge wings extend from the center of its

back toward its shoulders. The wings are

scythe-shaped, the inside is only partially visible, and

the bottom has jagged edges that almost make it

appear feathered. Its exquisite tail is covered in the same stone-like scales as its body and has a fan-like tip. If things couldn't get much worse, unfortunately it does. A thump of dirt, a flicker in the skies, and all of a sudden you are face to face with a hideous creature of ash and darkness. One flicker bursts from its gaping mouth with a most repulsive scent as another flicker's six vacant eyes stare at you with a dazed violence. Its broad head is covered in shadowy hair and a hood for the most part. The creature's chunky nose and twisted nostrils spew out magma. Its huge, sinewy body is perched on its large skull. The meaning of the strange tools or weapons that dangle at its side is, hopefully, a mystery.

The beast runs forward, its two legs carrying its devilish form with a dreadful grace. Behind it, a tail that resembles a tentacle crawls, with a barbed tip

wrapped in sticky slime at the end. Two enormous

wings spread out completely. Bones that resemble

scythes stretch upward before crashing down again

with great force. The monster sighs, turns its head

away from you, and stops recognizing you. It appears

to be the figure of Murphy as her true darkness

transforms her. Macauley's features as a horrible

screech, a flash of light, and all of a sudden you are

confronted by a monstrous monstrosity made of ash

and fear. A screech reverberates from its constricted

jaws in eerie joy as five ferocious eyes look at you

with a cruel fury.  Its bowed head, which is itself

fractured all over, is covered in a thick head of hair.

The creature's stubby nose and malformed nostrils

emit the sound of a roaring fire. Its tiny, hefty body

is perched above its bowed head. Although it appears to be enclosed by chains, you shouldn't really get too close to it to look it over more closely.

The thing moves forward with a step, its two legs carrying its dark body with a calm fury. The thing draws nearer and nearer, never taking its gaze off of you. The beasts of hell have risen and the lives of this world will never be the same again.

# Chapter 13

All that exists are patterns, patterns atop patterns, and patterns influencing other patterns. hidden patterns within patterns. within-pattern patterns. If you pay serious attention, history only ever repeats itself. Chaos is simply patterns we haven't noticed yet. What we consider random are only undecipherable patterns. What we don't grasp, we label as absurdity. We refer to non-readable text as gibberish. We have lost touch with chaos. This is the reason it has a negative reputation. Our world's main archetype, the Ego, clenches in terror of it since its existence is defined in terms of control. As it turns out, a spooky kind of order can appear to be in place, but deep within the order, a yet spooker kind of order can be found. Jackel Bunny and her demon misfits are wreaking havoc everywhere they go. I don't know how I was able to escape them, but I'm sure it won't be for long. Rudwick County has become a dead zone of bodies dropping dead and Syfer Keep is turning into that as we speak. I saw souls literally being sucked out of people's bodies and heads being ripped off and eaten. I'm going to try my best to get far away and regroup to hopefully find help with this crap. There has to be a way to stop this and send these demons back to hell where they belong. A bustling road that led to Syfer Keep was no longer discernible because nature had taken over the vacant space. The odd animal can be heard rustling in the overgrown shrubs or in the thick grasses of the neglected gardens. While some doorways appeared to be in quite good shape, others were completely ruined and couldn't be distinguished from other crumbling walls and heaps of debris. Drapes were occasionally thrown out by the wind, and window panes hung precariously from their hinges. Syfer Keep, once a peaceful, nice village with friendly residents, is now just a bitter memory. A once-vibrant village abounding in noises of joy and simple pleasures was now characterized by the wind in the trees and the creaking of wood. Over the years, the main hotel had hosted a few notable visitors, but it was now dilapidated and gradually beginning to crumble. A few creatures still venture here, but they prudently avoid the thin walls. No matter how you saw it, this town was a sinister sight. There was little anything left to show for it—lives that had been forgotten or possibly even utterly destroyed.

However, this community continued to perform its

role while no longer being what it once was. It was

still inhabited by a population, and life continued to

flourish there; except this time, it took the form of

animals. I was lucky enough to find a working car

when I escaped that house cabin. Driving on this

highway with no idea of where I wanna go is scary. It

feels like I have been driving for days, but it's only

been a couple hours and the sun will soon be up. I

need to find a motel or something to shower and get

some sleep. My mind and body is exhausted. I'm

emotionally stressed and I just need to eat and get

sleep. I make my way to a motel room after eating

chinese food. My eyes slowly fall into the darkness of

the back of my head. My body temples unto the bed

as I lie in peaceful harmony. So, I thought! I could see a vision of some sort showing me the town is covered in blood, guns, and shells. What was once a lovely farming hamlet is now the scene of an all-out invasion, and its new colors are red, brown, and silver.

The smell of gunpowder, blood, gore, and death has taken over the air, which would typically be filled with the aromas of food, fresh fish, and new brews, making even the most courageous quiver in horror. Tragically, both the environment and humanity are suffering. Years will most certainly pass before this town has fully healed. It is obvious that destroyed siege engines, explosion craters, and rubble have replaced the businesses, gardens, and other structures. I could feel my body sweating through the night. It was as if I was paralyzed in my slumber, because I can't move. I could now see my own body laying on the bed as if I'm awake in this vision world again. It's dark in this room obviously since I'm supposed to be asleep. I don't know how I am seeing my own body sleep. Walking in the distance of my body trying to see if I can reach out to myself. Dizziness began to roll over me in this realm and I can no longer hold on. As I was falling down to the ground, out the corner of my eyes I could see a red burnt hand opening a white claw. A man of some sort with a red burnt face and shades is sitting at my table drinking. Laughing at me with his sharp teeth showing out of his mouth.  If you aren't eliminating your opponents, it's because you have already been subjugated and assimilated; you have no idea who they are. Your mind has been made to believe that you are your own worst adversary, and you are determined to defeat yourself. While you are tearing yourself apart, the adversary is laughing at you. Confounding your enemies is the most effective form of warfare an enemy can use against you. Only bombs may be used to disseminate an idea. Using either real or love bombs (manipulation). There is a distinction between an instinct that cannot be resisted and an impulse that is not resisted. And for this reason, the best thieves avoid capture. We must not allow the thought to cross our minds that an argument might not be valid. However, we must gird ourselves and make every effort to improve our health despite the fact that we are still intellectually defective. The development of a hatred for debate is the worst possible outcome for anyone. Mind is avaricious. The mind abandons those views and leans toward those people only to reap maximum benefits when you sense the benefits from those who had previously had negative opinions of you. On the ground as I am I can hear Sabrina's ratched voice laughing at me again. Her voice said to me, "We got you again…. Little bitch thought she was free." I don't know what could be going on. Is this a trap again…. What is happening?

# Chapter 14

I am waking up in a dizzy way as I can't move my body, but everything else around me is moving. I realize I am chained up on a carrier of some sort and I see people around holding each handle. The little I can see it seems as if this is a dungeon I am in right now. The entry to this dungeon is a small, dim tunnel in a dark swamp. Beyond the dim cave is a large, soggy space. Rubble, cobwebs, and rat droppings are all over it. You can view tripped traps and skeleton remains that have been damaged and destroyed by time itself thanks to your torch. You take the left of the three roads that are further ahead. You continue along the trail's winding path until you get to a worn-out spot. There are several traps, axes in motion, and other gadgets throughout.

They have either recently activated or are still active.

What transpired in this location? You keep going,

moving deeper into the shadows of the dungeon.

Many of the rooms and corridors you pass either go

nowhere or circle back to the same place. Finally, you

reach what is probably the last room. A large wooden

door stands in your way. It is covered with intricate

carvings that have remained unspoiled by time and

the elements. You move in closer to examine it when

you hear a knock on the door. "You got the girl

finally to shut up?" A female voice says as the door

opens. "Yes we did and now we can have some more

fun." Sabrina Jackel responds. She continues, "Right

now we have her in a way of thinking she's in a

motel or something. She thinks she got away, but she

is only trapped deeper in her own head." The female

voice responds, "My father has taught you well I see

and you listened to apply. Well done." Sabrina with

gratitude, "Thank you, her majesty Katiee

Powell-Corpse, Princess demon of hell." Princess

Katiee smiles, but confesses. "But there is one thing

my father hasn't told you yet. There is more to the

reasoning of why he wants Amya so much." She

exclaims more, "Hell Amya doesn't even know who

she is, she doesn't even know her parents weren't her

real parents at all. They spent years having her

memories be suppressed, because they were terrified

of the kind of power she has in her." Sabrina, Chris,

Macauley, Malacki and Murphy are all stunned by

the revelation that has been spoken. "What could be

so powerful within this blonde, skinny, pale skinned

chick exactly?" Chris laughs as he speaks, but gets

slapped in the face by Princess Katiee. "What the

hell!! Why did you slap me?" Chris reacts out of

anger. "Bro probably, because you're being an idiot

and disrespecting a woman. Just, because we may be

doing dealings with a demon, even they have respect

for treating women right."

A work's inherent potency cannot ever be kept secret

or locked away. A piece of art may be rejected,

forbidden, or forgotten by the passage of time, but

the essential will always win out over the transient.

Before we are compelled to reveal our hidden

strength, we aren't even aware of it. People go above

and beyond in times of sorrow, conflict, and

necessity. The ability of humans to survive and grow

is amazing. When we face challenges, we discover

courage and resiliency that we never knew we possessed. And it's only until we experience failure that we realize we've always had these resources within us. All we have to do is locate them so we can continue living. Your capacity for flexibility and adaptation will enable you to remain open to all of the hidden benefits that struggle may provide, regardless of the turns and turns your life may take. Life's goal is to follow the secret directive that assures everyone is in harmony and builds a world that is getting better all the time. We weren't made just to appreciate the planet; the universe needs us to advance it. I could understand everything they were saying about me. About some hidden power within me, but what power do I have in me that scares the corpse fiend. My parents weren't my real parents.

Where am I from and how am I on earth? So many

questions went through my mind, but I still couldn't

fully process what was going on. I could see a fiery

sharp knife they were about to stab me with. Chants

are being made, but I can't hear what is being said.

My chest was radiating with fire. In an effort to end

this torment, a fist clamped into my skin, its claws

piercing the skin deeply. It will all be over soon

enough, I was certain. Pain couldn't possibly last that

long, would it? I had a moment of panic when I

realized I might be wrong. It took me a moment or

two to regain control, but conflicting ideas were still

running rampant through my head. I tightly closed

my eyes, and a grimace appeared on my face. My

only choice was to try to swallow the agony and

ignore it. The best course of action, in my opinion,

was to just cope with it and get on with life till the pain decreased because there didn't seem to be much that could be done in either direction. An internal voice is the final narrator of our endearing and enduring personal tale or the documentarian of our sad and disgusting plotlines, so we must carefully cultivate the voice that speaks to us. We construct our functional reality from the stories we tell ourselves, and this format creates the concourse of the layered emotional control panel that steers and braces us through the clamor of the present. If words were to be said, they would come from the other side of the wall. Distance and travel time from this minute on are unaccountable. If words need to be spoken, they should be impressed through the wall in ever-so-slightly increments to the opposite side's signature, hearing, speech, and grip. The voices in my head were always supposed to be heard, welcomed, and transformed into something as intriguing as poetry. They were never meant to be hushed. I want to say at this point that the voice occupies space in two ways. It actively seeks out space for itself as well as inhabiting and occupying it. Because the voice is space, the voice occurs in space. When a doubt develops, I've seen that there are always two voices stating opposing opinions. Always. A decision must be made. Another thing I've seen is that when two voices shout, one usually chooses the one that is nearest to their hearts.

# Chapter 15

Not this again!!! It appears I have made it to another realm, but something feels different here. It's not dark or scary in this place. I don't know if I am dying and I am in the inbetween or something else. A variety of bushes and shrubs surround an unkempt stretch of grass. The pagoda, which is surrounded by lovely, flowering vines, is situated close to the garden's left side. Although the flowers and plants may need some TLC, they are still alive and draw attention. The bushes and shrubs develop to a height of 1.2 m (4 ft), but they will keep growing until they are either halted or fall over under their own weight. Every bend in the garden is encircled by a path made of stepping stones that invites guests to explore its most attractive areas. In an effort to increase their own dominance, grass and plants are beginning to retake even the most remote areas of land.

Even from the opposite side of the garden, one may enjoy the pagoda. You can't win when the garden is planned around the pagoda; the flowers and plants shouldn't be neglected, and the bushes and shrubs shouldn't be denied their fair share of attention. As I walk through this garden realm, I see a woman in the distance in white and orange. "Hello! Hello!" I screamed out to her as if it was my last breath. I feel so weakened I fell to one knee and began to spill blood out of my mouth. My life force is shedding away from me as we speak. "You must tap into your power Amya." An unknown voice says to me as I spit blood. "Who is there that is speaking to me?" I asked with grief. It was the woman in white and orange as she raised my chin up. "Look at me my darling….You are not alone. I am with you as I've always been. You must defeat this evil and gain your power. My name is Stiletta and I am your mother you didn't get to know long ago. Now take my hand and embrace the power I pass upon you as the demon slayer warrior."

As I embrace the power transfer there is this suit of armor featuring a hood and a facial guard that seems amused. Two expertly carved faces, one crying and the other laughing, are fastened to one of its sides.

The shoulders are tiny, slender, and pointed. Three lines of spikes that are straight and extend from side to side embellish them. Under the shoulderplates, loose-fitting rerebraces that are squared and completely encircle the upper arms provide protection. Vambraces that have layers of handmade leather that resemble dragon scales cover the lower arms.

Numerous layers of v-shaped leather and fur are sewn together to form the breastplate, which also has decorative parts and rounded edges. It simply covers the front; the attachment straps, which are in the rear and don't really provide any protection, are there. A skirt made of horizontal layers of leather and fur that extends to the knees covers the upper legs. Leather shin guards with a dagger attached to the outside protect the lower legs. Under this, thick furry pants are worn. In the midst of my armor transformation I asked my mother, "What am I? Do we have a certain name for us?" Out of her mouth I could hear one thing and it was, " Geranalone " As the Jackel Bunny cult and Princess Demon Katiee were doing their ritual upon me. My body burst into fire as flames rose out of my eyes and mouth like a dragon. "What the fuck is this? Was this a part of the ritual?" Murphy asks as everyone gets blasted away and I am back to my full strength. Demon Katiee with all her might stares at me and says, "Shit! This can't be I thought you Geranalone's died a long time ago." Everyone around looks at Princess Katiee and says "A what?" Chris screams, "I didn't sign up for any of this. I am out of here." Chris, Macauley, Malacki and Murphy all run for their lives and leave Sabrina Jackel alone. Princess Katiee uses her powers and is transported back to hell where she belongs. It is preferable to defeat yourself than to triumph in a thousand conflicts. The triumph is then yours. You cannot have it taken away from you by angels, demons, heaven, or hell. There are countless devils, and they always show up when it's least convenient, terrifying people. But I've discovered that I can use the opposing forces to my advantage if I can control them and harness them for my chariot. Your demons will deal with you if you don't, and it's going to hurt. A memoir makes me pause and pay close attention to my memories. It is a test of honesty. In a memoir, I examine my life, my loved ones, and myself in the reflection of the empty page. In a memoir, emotions are more significant than facts, and I must face my problems in order to write honestly. Every person possesses monsters and demons. They serve as metaphors for the state of humanity. Rebounds are definitely not simple. The most challenging element of recovering from major surgery is overcoming inner demons. Everything is in the mind. Only a person can conquer his fears. As people, we have dark sides and dark difficulties to deal with. You must confront your demons if you want to advance in life. We make a lot of effort to filter off unfavorable or troubling thoughts, but occasionally facing your demons is the most energizing action you can take. You're constantly looking for the thing that would help you heal, and I believed counseling would provide that for me. But it didn't; all it does is make your demons more apparent.I've frequently pondered what else I might have been, like many other individuals. Even after I stopped being a child, I still believed that Batman was the total deal when I was younger. intelligent, logical, and practical. Depressed but in a way that attracted women. a tragic person at heart who is battling his demons while attempting to save the world. Geche Gimpia is a defensive and offensive martial art that emphasizes defeating your adversary with incredibly accurate and well-timed attacks. The main emphasis is on blocks and grapples, and it frequently depends on your own stamina and your opponent's strength. Geche Gimpia's remarkable close-range power and quickness are his greatest assets. You can take full advantage of the tendency of your opponent to overexert oneself by using your own side steps.

# Chapter 16

As Sabrina and I are tearing each other a part in this dungeon I can sense her beginning to be weak. With everyone gone including Demon Katiee, the jackel bunny seems to be very vulnerable. I never would have imagined in a million years that I would know martial arts. The world appeared to be spinning around Sabrina as she gulped for air and wobbled on her feet. At times, the anguish receded only to return with what seemed to be greater intensity. She briefly considered everything she may lose if she gave in to the pain, as well as everything that might result from it. It was getting more and harder to endure the pain, but it was also getting more and more frustrating to have to. I can obviously tell that her body has been broken. Sabrina is able to lay there even though a body shouldn't be able to. So this will be the last she does. With no one to aid her, she is warped and twisted.

Although she knows she can't, she still thinks she can get through this. This situation is completely hopeless. I am certain that she will pass away. But she doesn't want to; she wants to live, not die. She begs me to save her, but I take the decisive action of ripping off her head and setting it ablaze with the fire coming from my mouth. I set fire to everything in this dungeon so it will no longer exist. This stuff is over; no more tricks or lies will be tolerated.

However, I still have unfinished business and people I want to exact revenge on. Revenge... is like a rolling stone that, after a man pushes it up a hill, will come back at him with more power and crush the bones

that its sinews propelled. The alternating rule of one

side over another, heightened by the spirit of

vengeance inherent in party strife, which in various

eras and nations has committed the most horrifying

enormities, is in and of itself a dreadful despotism.

However, this eventually results in a more formal

and long-lasting tyranny. Without justice, the most

horrific crimes go unpunished; victims cannot

receive compensation; and peace remains a distant

objective because impunity breeds more animosity,

which results in retaliatory acts and increased

suffering. Because of man's insatiable desire to wreak

revenge for his hatred, evil always conjures up new

forms of destructive pain. I don't know how my next

journey will fold, but what I do know is that I won't

be weak this time. Evil never stops and Chris,

Malacki, and those other two earned what they have

coming from me. They had an easy target at first,

but things have changed now. I'm not this weak

twenty something year old girl in college anymore.

College is overrated anyway. No matter how far they

may get I am going to find them and all the evil

that's out there. Due to its cheap construction, this

weapon is not only lauded for being wonderful but

also infamous globally.

The weapon's normal length is 736mm, its barrel is

412mm, and its weight is around 4.4kg.

Although it can come in a wide range of different

calibers, it uses 7.62x35mm bullets. For easier and

less expensive prospective maintenance, the weapon

includes an upper and lower receiver. Depending on

your preferences, the pistol grip can also be made of

ivory or an exotic wood in addition to metal.

While various stock materials are sadly still

unavailable, the stock is manufactured of maple. The

straight grip stock is a close second in terms of

popularity to the full grip stock, which is the

industry standard. There are various magazines

available in addition to the STANAG standard issue

magazine, which holds 50 rounds. The magazine can

be released using both a button and a lever system.

Two-round burst, automatic, and safe mode are the

selectable fire modes. To combat emerging dangers,

this weapon was developed for the covert forces. An

Asian man named Tan the Man created it.

A civilian version of this weapon is most certainly

out of the question, albeit there are quite a few

different variations that are already in production or soon will be. The weapon's official name is the 2I-7K, however it is more often known as "Bulldog Lizzy." This sturdy steel teardrop kite shield provides a powerful defense, especially against knife and small-ballistic attacks. This is the result of skill, as orcs worked in a chronomatic forge to craft this shield. The margins of the shield have been given a scaly appearance and reinforced with layered metal scales. Zealous writing and symmetrical paints embellish its center. This shield has undoubtedly experienced triumph and glory. There may be signs left by who knows what, such as nicks and slashes, that suggest you should stay away from its master's route, but one thing is certain: this shield is ravenous. When looking for a little extra security, civilians frequently choose this tiny revolver. It's not difficult to manage because of its counterbalanced weight. It boasts a decent amount of firepower and excellent accuracy. This specific revolver has an ivory grip, horn ornamentation, a pricey metal barrel that could be gilded, and ivory and horn accents. This weapon was first intended to be an alternative to another weapon, but it quickly expanded into a massive mass production endeavor and is now used by both gangs and civil authorities.

Although it is most frequently referred to by its informal name: Moe. This remarkable rifle crossbow has been skillfully built from remarkably durable timber. Prime bear sinew, a material that is extremely scarce in certain parts of the world, is used to make its string. The limbs finish in curves that resemble wings and are embellished with numerous

little spikes. The stock is adorned with magic runes

and wrapped in silky silk. The little quiver is

designed to be wrapped around the archer's back and

is made of reptile skin. Gilded ornaments on the

exterior have been added, maybe to commemorate

prior victories. A skilled archer may use this bow to

fire arrows up to 123 meters away while maintaining

lethal force.

# Chapter 17

Ten tall, square towers, joined by high, solid walls of light green stone, dwarf everything beneath them. In addition to symmetric holes for artillery and archers, the walls also have narrow, asymmetrical rows of rough windows. All those in need in these chilly mountains have a safe haven provided by a large gate with impressive wooden doors, a drawbridge, and archer holes, but there are other entrances if you know where to look for the castle's hidden corridors. The exterior of the castle is decorated with well-kept scorched gardens of lava, horrifying trees, and many severed skins. Even though it has experienced some extremely trying periods, this castle has withstood the test of time in hell and appears to be able to endure for many more years. "She has failed me once more and I will not have it any longer." Corpse Fiend says in his castle, banging on his throne of fire. Demon Princess Katiee arrives back to her father and seeks to know the next move. "Father she has gotten her powers and I fear there could be more to be discovered. What shall you have me do?" The Corpse Fiend contemplates with heavy breath.... "She may have won this battle, but the war has yet begun. I have seen the potential futures and I must not let her come into her full self." Katiee responds, "Her full self father.... What perhaps do you mean?" Corpse Fiend looks with his concerned red eyes to say, "She only discovered a piece of her power as her full power has not yet activated."

There will come a moment when the ground is covered in blood, injured soldiers, and suits. What was once a peaceful land has now been transformed into the scene of a horrific war, with red, black, and gray serving as its new colors.

There is no turning back from this; the air, which would ordinarily be filled with the sounds of nature, is now a horrible symphony of cries, explosions, and gunfire. Due to a treachery, two armies engage in combat, although it is still unclear which side will prevail. The faces of the combatants are hopeful as they carry out their orders in a bloody battle as the bodies and wounded of one side are strewn across the land. The opposing side fights with a mixture of confidence and panic, which is appropriate given that their lives do. Others appear to be relatively unfazed by the terrors going on around them, while

some have succumbed to fright and are no longer

able to move, much less protect themselves. Both the

environment and humans are suffering greatly. It

will probably be a while before this land to fully

recover. It would be obvious that where there once

were plants, flowers, and shrubs, there are now

explosion holes, metal, and rubble. The prophet will

bring about a period of peace and an age of death

when the rivers run dry. When the last one is reborn,

a heinous crime will cause blue blood to spill and a

golden age to begin. The guilty will usher in an era

of chaos and the eradication of culture on the day

that the wolves howl together. The guilty will usher

in a time of justice and misery on the day that what

is blue turns red. Large, dense, and varied

described the forest. Redwood, crab apple, and asp clambered for its canopy, and there were enough gaps for a mix of sprouts to claim the boulder-covered lands below.

Most trees had curved limbs hanging from them, and the sporadic scattering of flowers gave the otherwise monochromatic scene some color.

The forest was alive with a variety of sounds, most of which were made by animals, and they blended well with the splashing of fish in a nearby lake. There were endless fields, barely broken up by a river that wound and swirled through the countryside. Cows and lambs were sleeping and grazing all around you in the peaceful pastures, and a stone road was running through the many fields.

The pathway led to a massive mansion that was totally obscured by the lush pergola adjacent to it. The home was in wonderful shape overall, but it needed a fresh coat of paint. Numerous bee hives were located behind the main buildings, a sizable stable housed a large number of horses, and a modest seating area offered a spot to rest while taking in some of the farm-produced goods. The warm sun rays and the pleasant breeze were the main causes of the farm's homey atmosphere.

What once was a t-shirt is now a ruffled mess of frayed threads, stains, and holes; it just about manages to hang from my shoulders like a used old towel. Much of my is now exposed to the elements because a significant portion of the right side has been torn off and there are holes everywhere.

I'm covering my t-shirt with a tough poncho. Even though it is ripped, stained, and covered in grease, it at least keeps me somewhat wind-protected. My clothes are also a complete mess. These jeans are now a filth-stained pile of shreds due to tears and rips. But at least my feet are covered by shoes. Even though they are torn, the right shoe's outer sole has long since disappeared, and it is a size too small. A tiny scarf that I'm wearing around my neck is tucked under my nose and wrapped over my face. Even though it's filthy and subpar, at least it doesn't smell. A bandana that covers my head has a few minor holes here and there, but overall it's clean and in good shape. Rare flower bushes edge a grassy area filled with moss. A greenhouse with a variety of fruits, veggies, and more exotic flowers is located in the garden's back right corner. The smaller flower

bushes are thriving and proud, getting all their

needs met by the garden; they serve as a stopover for

bees. The flower bushes don't get much taller than

1.5 meters (5 feet), though. The garden is circled by a

single path marked by round stones that nearly

takes visitors by the hand while pointing out the best

vistas. The only tools that can stop plants, grass, and

roots from claiming the entire garden as their own

are sheers, trimmers, and mowers. The greenhouse

commands everyone's attention, which also focuses

attention on everything nearby. Nothing compares to

the grandeur of the greenhouse, despite the smaller

flower bushes' best efforts to steal some of the

spotlight and their typically stunning appearances.

Outside, my residence appears to be cozy. It has white

pine wooden ornamentation and was constructed

with blue stones. A rather uneven pattern of tall,

huge windows has been added to the house, adding

to its overall appearance.

The home contains two bedrooms, a comfortable

living room, a big dining room, a vast storage room,

as well as an outdated kitchen and one modern

bathroom. The structure has a rectangular shape. A

covered patio encircles the home on two sides, in

part. Due to the second floor's lesser size than the

first, the home's sides may accommodate numerous

balconies. Compared to the floor below, this floor has

a radically different aesthetic. Brown roof tiles cover

the tall, triangular, multi-layered roof. The home has

two sizable chimneys on either side of it. There are

no windows on the roof. A small, secure yard with a

playground in the middle and a majority of it made of grass surrounds the home itself. I have made my own secluded plantation out here in Union, Maine. It's really beautiful here and I find peace here. Plus I'm going to need a peacekeeping place to come back to after my revenge spree. I've been here for the last year and I think I've given those assholes enough time to live out their final moments before I come for them. I got everything set up like I wanted it to be and I hired a private cleaner to watch it out for me while I'm gone. This magnificent Union, Maine, city. This union, which was founded on the camaraderie, abundant nature, and rare resources of its history, is now one of the most hazardous nations in its region of the world.

Among its current strongest points are their

industry, literacy, and public health. Unfortunately,

they have significant education and fuel efficiency

gaps. The union in Union, Maine is patriarchal.

There are no opposition organizations to the current

leadership, but there once were.

The nation is currently most in danger from an

active volcano, but the current administration lacks

the resources to address this problem. I'll just say

that Union, Maine residents are struggling with

depression. They lead bleak lives, but despite the

industry's poor fuel efficiency, some of their

problems are alleviated.

Their lives are completely unaffected by religion,

which if anything has boosted their self-assurance.

However, the people of Union are quite cohesive, and

they have many festivals and old customs. A startling explosion of fire and a rumbling in the sky are followed by a sickening entity made of flame and blood. Another rumble emanates from its horrifying mouth in a fit of wrath as its six bright eyes fix you with an agonizing resentment.

Its stout head, which is itself dimly gleaming in the dark, is adorned with two curled horns. The creature's loose nostrils, positioned within a large nose, let out a plume of smoke.

Its massive, sinewy body is atop a stout head. The creature seemed to take pride in the large scar that crossed its chest.

The creature dashes in your direction, its six legs carrying its cursed body with grace and a calm aura.

Two flimsy wings spread out completely. Shadow

feathers and skin-covered bones reach skyward as though attempting to fully block you. Every second, the creature's threatening glare intensifies. I wondered how long it was going to be until that Corpse fiend was going to come after me. I see one demon so far, but I know there are soon more to be behind it. You find yourself face-to-face with a respectable beast of filth and embers after hearing a howl in the dark and some wood breaking. Another roar rages from its wide mouth in incomprehensible agony, and four flaming eyes look at you with a terrible obsession.

Its rough skull, which itself is always grinning, is adorned with two jagged horns. The monster has deep nostrils set within a gaunt snout, and its breath is foul.

A huge, hulking torso rests atop its rough skull. Who knows the significance of the cloak that covers its torso, which is weirdly beautiful. The monster sprints forward, its four legs carrying its wretched body with ease and a serene vigor. Behind it, a blade-like tail that is entirely covered with runes moves. The creature's stare, which hasn't once left yours, seems to be disappointed. As soon as I rushed to grab my weapons from my barn, my skull was being pulsed with sharp, tearing pain. I had a heavy feeling in my brain, and I was beginning to feel lightheaded. I looked for every possible solution in my desperate need for relief. ignoring it, pushing through it, and using it as strength-building fuel. But nothing appeared to be working. At this point, it would presumably only take a straightforward decision to give up or continue, but the decision just didn't seem to come. My legs could hardly support me, and everything around me seemed to be spinning erratically light. The best course of action, in my opinion, was to just cope with it and get on with life till the pain decreased because there didn't seem to be much that could be done in either direction. It stings! It stings so bad! I'm at my limit here! Someone needs to stop it! I can't. It is too heavy for me to move. My arms weigh too much. Someone, somebody put a stop to it.

My body is immobile, and I am even unable to move my head. All I can do is stare up at the sky while I wait to die. At least the sky is lovely, I suppose.

No! I'm not leaving like this, not at all! That's impossible! I'm more capable than this; this is sad. I can overcome this. Yes, I will leave this place; I

simply have to figure out how. That shouldn't be that

challenging. I'm very exhausted. I am unable to give

in and stay up, though. Sleeping means I'll die, thus I

must fight to live. But my body is exhausted; perhaps

I should take a little nap to conserve my energy till

assistance arrives. That would be ideal, of course.

Save my power. Soon, help will arrive. I will perish. I

regret not seeing snippets of my life as I

progressively deteriorate like in the movies. Maybe

they haven't arrived yet. Though I know I don't have

much time left, it should happen soon. Better get

ready for the performance. I have lost all feeling in

my body, including my arms and legs. absolutely

nothing. At least I don't feel any pain, so that's

somewhat comforting. I have no feelings at all.

Focusing was challenging since I was experiencing agony and hearing voices urging me to quit what I was doing, but I must continue. I can't let this scumbag triumph. These idiots cannot possess my soul. I'll go after my revenge and exact it. Why are my abilities not active? This cannot be correct. However, after a few more intensely focused seconds, I was able to block out the pain to the point that it was no more than a slight irritation. They'll manage, but it'll take some time. As I am stuck to the ground out of my rear eye view I could see Sabrina once again. She walks to me laughing at my pain and says, "You didn't think this was over did you? No... no..no the party is just getting started."

To be continued.......

Jackel Bunny and Amya fitzgerald will return